While
The Bear Sleeps

For Leila and Gabriel — C. M.
For Samuel — J. C. M.

Barefoot Collections
an imprint of
Barefoot Books
37 West 17th Street
4th Floor East
New York, New York 10011

This book has been printed on 100% acid-free paper
The illustrations were prepared in acrylic on medium thick illustration board

Graphic design by Jennie Hoare, England
This book was typeset in Minion 13pt
Color separation by Unifoto, Cape Town
Printed and bound in Singapore by Tien Wah Press (Pte) Ltd

1 3 5 7 9 8 6 4 2

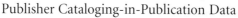

Publisher Cataloging-in-Publication Data

Matthews, Caitlín.
    While the bear sleeps : winter tales and
traditions / retold by Caitlín Matthews ;
illustrated by Judith Christine Mills.—1st ed.
[80]p. : col. ill. ;   cm.
Includes bibliographical references.
Summary: The adventures of a young girl as she
travels through time with a bear as her guide;
discovering the origins of winter tales and traditions
from the first snowfall to the return of spring..
ISBN 1-902283-81-3
1. Night -- Fiction -- Juvenile literature. 2. Tales. I. Mills, Judith, ill.
II. Title.
   [F]--dc21 1999   AC   CIP

While The Bear Sleeps

Winter Tales and Traditions

Retold by
CAITLÍN MATTHEWS

Illustrated by
JUDITH CHRISTINE MILLS

BAREFOOT BOOKS

Contents

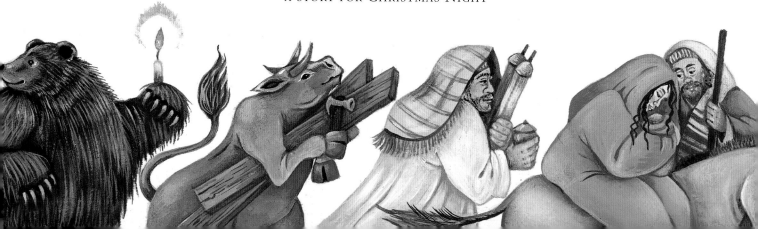

WHILE *the* BEAR SLEEPS

ONCE UPON A TIME, there was a girl who went out into the hills just as it was beginning to snow. It became very cold and she found a deep hole in the side of the rock. She climbed inside and pulled grass and branches over the entrance to keep out the snow. Inside it was warm and snug, but completely dark.

Suddenly a deep voice asked sleepily, "Didn't your mother tell you not to go into the bear's den?"

"Is this what this hole is?" asked the girl.

"Certainly," said the voice. "But seeing as it's so cold outside, you might as well stay here with me and sleep. I generally do that when winter comes."

"Why?" asked the girl.

"Because it's the time when you look inside yourself and remember the important things."

"What are they?" asked the girl.

"That the winter is never so cold when you can share stories with the friends of your heart. That loneliness is never so lonely if you are used to being alone. That you need never worry about how you look or what people think about you if you are at home to yourself. That's why I come here."

"And do you have friends of your heart in this cave?" asked the girl.

"Oh yes," said the bear. "Curl up beside me and sleep, and you will meet some of them."

For although the girl did not realize it, she had stepped into the cave of a rather special bear. While they slept, he visited her in her dreams. With him she traveled to many faraway places; and from him she learned many of the tales and traditions that mark the winter months…

WHO WAS ST. NICHOLAS?

"WHERE ARE WE?" asked the girl. As she rubbed her eyes and looked around, she realized that she was in strange clothes. It was nighttime, and very dark, but she could tell that she was in a city of some kind. In the moonlight she saw a strange figure climbing up to the window of a nearby house and throwing in some sacks.

"Who is he?" she whispered to the bear.

"Hush, child! That is St. Nicholas, the man your people now call Santa Claus. They say he lives in the North Pole, but in the beginning he lived in Lycia. That is where we are."

"Where is Lycia?"

"It is in one of the great continents, the continent of Asia; but the place matters less than the deed. Do you know what the man is doing? He is helping a poor merchant; a widower who has three daughters. The merchant has lost his fortune, and Nicholas is secretly giving the family some sacks of money."

"Oh look!" cried the girl. "Someone is trying to catch him!"

"That is the merchant. Nicholas did not want him to wake up, but he has. So now he knows where the money has come from. Soon many others will know too. Nicholas is the bishop of this region, and he is already famous far and wide for his acts of kindness. That is why he will soon be made a saint. He will become the patron saint of all children and his feast will be celebrated every year on December 5."

"Is he the same person as Santa Claus?"

"He is and he is not. Hold my paw and close your eyes."

"That's Santa Claus, on the top of that house, with his ear to the chimney!" cried the girl. "But who is the man that is with him?"

"Yes, that is Santa Claus, or Sinterklass, as he is known here. Now we are in the Netherlands, in northern Europe. The people here gave St. Nicholas his new name. He is with his helper, Black Piet or Peter, and he is listening hard at the chimney to find out how the children below are behaving. Black Peter has a birch rod for naughty children, and the sack bearing the presents of Sinterklass for the good children can be used for carrying away the bad children when it's empty! Let's go inside the house. The children are putting their shoes near the fire and singing."

Nicholas, I beg of you,
Drop into my little shoe,
Something sweet or sweeter.
Thank you, Saint and Peter.
Nicholas, please remember,
On the fifth of December,
Fill my little shoe,
All for love of you.

"Do you know what the sweetest gift of midwinter is, little one? Listen carefully, and before you leave my cave you may have found out! But now it is time for our first story. It is a winter's tale from Russia."

The WINTER CABIN

~A STORY FOR THE FIRST SNOWFALL~

There was once an old peasant called Josef who kept a pig, a rooster, a ram, a goose and an ox. There were guests coming for dinner that Sunday and so Josef called to his wife, "We will need some meat. I'll kill the rooster tomorrow."

The rooster heard these words and quietly hid in the forest. When Josef went to wring the bird's neck, the rooster had vanished. "So, I can't find the rooster! I shall have to kill the pig instead!" said Josef to his wife.

The pig looked up from her trough and ran squealing into the forest. Next day Josef looked everywhere for her in vain. "No rooster, no pig — how very strange! Well, I shall just have to kill the ram instead."

The ram overheard this and went to the goose, saying, "I'm off to the forest and, if you're wise, you'll go too." And so off they went.

Next day Josef scoured the yard for the ram and the goose, without success. "Well, wife, it looks as though we shall have to slaughter the ox, since none of the other beasts can be found."

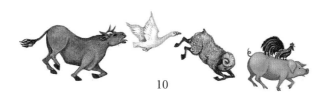

But the ox was soon off as fast as his legs could carry him. The animals lived happily in the forest that summer, eating whatever they liked, free to roam without a care in the world. But summer soon turned to fall and fall brought the cold winds and the first ice.

"Listen, friends," said the ox. "Winter is coming and we must seek shelter if we are to survive. The old man isn't going to come out here and thatch the branches of the trees to keep us dry and warm, you know. We must build a winter cabin for ourselves."

The ram said, "My thick woolly coat will keep me warm."

The pig said, "I shall dig a big hole and lie snug in the earth."

"My soft feathers will be like a quilt against the cold," said the goose.

"I can manage by roosting in a tree," said the rooster.

When the ox saw that none of the animals could be bothered to help him, he set to and made a winter cabin out of wood. Inside he put a stove of stone and made his bed on top of it. Only a few days later, fall turned to winter. The winds sent down the first snows and the animals in the forest began to look for shelter.

The ram's fleecy coat was soon hung with icicles and he banged with his horns on the door of the winter cabin. "Brrrr, brrrr! Let me in!" he called.

From within the cozy cabin, the ox said, "You didn't want to help me when I asked. You said your thick coat would keep you warm."

"Let me in, or I shall break down the door with my horns."

"Goodness! I shall be cold without a door," thought the ox, and he let the ram inside to warm himself on the bench beside the stove.

Soon the pig was at the door, her pink skin all pimply with cold. "Oink-woink! Won't you let me in to warm myself?"

"I will not!" replied the ox. "You said that you would keep warm by burrowing in the earth; you didn't want to help me."

"If you don't let me in, I shall dig under the walls and the hut will fall down," said the pig.

"Dear me!" thought the ox. "Then we will be cold indeed." And he opened the door to let the pig inside. Down she went into the cellar where she curled up contentedly.

Next came the goose, her white feathers looking even paler with a covering of snowflakes upon them. "Garak, garak! Let me come in!" she honked.

"But you said that your soft feathers would feel as warm as a quilt!" said the ox.

"If you don't let me in, I shall peck all the moss from the cracks in the windows."

"Now that won't do," thought the ox. "There are enough drafts in this house already with me opening the door so much."

And he let in the goose, who came and roosted on the post by the door.

Lastly the rooster came, with his feathers all blown about and sticking up like twigs. "Corrock-cor-oo! Let me come in!" he demanded.

"I thought you were going to spend the winter in a tree," said the ox.

"If you don't let me in, I shall scratch holes in the roof. Let me in now."

"We don't want the snow coming in," thought the ox. And he let in the rooster, who fluttered up to settle on a beam over the door.

And there the animals stayed in their winter cabin.

The winter grew colder and the snow deeper. Soon other visitors were planning to visit, hungry visitors who wanted to eat the five friends. In the heart of the forest a pack of wolves drew lots to see who would go into the winter cabin first. A wily old gray wolf won.

With his clever paws, the wolf was quick to open the cabin door. But his visit was not at all what he expected! As soon as he was inside, the ox pinned him bodily to the wall with his long horns. The ram butted him in the side and the pig squeaked up from the cellar in a bloodthirsty way, "Skroink-woink! I'm sharpening the ax and the knife, ready to skin you alive!"

The goose rushed in and nipped the wolf very painfully on his behind, while the rooster danced overhead screeching out, "Give him to me. I'll slit his throat and hang him from the beam over the door."

The other wolves, who had been listening at the door, took to their heels in terror. The wily old gray wolf twisted and turned and yelped and scratched as he struggled to free himself. Leaving a great patch of fur between the ox's horns, he leaped away from the winter cabin with his tail between his legs. Never had he been so beaten up.

When he had rejoined his pack, the wolf related his adventures. "I tell you, friends, there are five monsters in that cabin! There was a huge peasant in a black shirt who knocked the breath out of me and set about my head with clubs. Then there was a small, gray-coated fiend who punched me all over. A furious demon in a white cloak knocked nails into my behind, while a fearsome villain in a scarlet cap kept threatening to hang me up. As for the one who was sharpening the knives and axes to skin me, I shudder to think what he must have looked like!"

From that day on, the pack of wolves left the winter cabin and its monstrous occupants very much alone. And the ox, rooster, ram, goose and pig lived peacefully together that winter.

LIGHT IN THE DARKNESS

"Are there bears in Russia?"

"Oh yes. We are not as many as we were, mind you. But that is the same for many animals whose lives have been sacrificed and whose homes have been destroyed by human greed. We are pretty safe at this time of the year, though. We bears sleep right through the dark months of winter and no one is much inclined to disturb us because it is too cold."

"What makes it so cold and dark in winter?"

"From midsummer to midwinter the sun gradually moves away from the northern lands. That is why the days grow so much shorter and the weather turns cold. So people need fire to keep them warm. Before the days of electricity, it was too dark to work on winter nights, so everyone loved to sit by the fire and exchange stories. Many of those stories are about light; and light is the main theme of many midwinter festivals.

"Can you imagine this earth without light? We need the light of the sun for many things. Without it, plants could not grow; without it, all the birds and animals, all the fishes and plants and people would die of cold and hunger; without it, no one would be able to see. Of course, we need the darkness too; but what would happen if the sun disappeared? People have asked that question for more years than anyone can remember.

"So every flame, every candle that people light, is like a little sun. It is a spark of light that promises the return of the warm, growing seasons of spring and summer. It also reminds us that we need to learn to see deeply into the mysteries of life. We need to understand how every living thing has its place and deserves to be treated with honor and respect.

"'Lucia' is a girl's name, but do you know what it means? It means 'light.' In Sweden people remember St. Lucia on December 13 each year."

"What did she do to become a saint?"

"She was a Christian girl who was captured by the Roman emperor Diocletian. At that time, Christians had to worship in secret, so they went to pray in caves at night. Lucia would visit them with food so they would not go hungry. To enable her to carry as much food as possible with both hands, she would light her way in the dark with a crown of candles. One day she was caught and killed. In remembrance of St. Lucia, it is the custom in Sweden for the youngest daughter to wake up early on December 13 and put on a long white dress with a red sash, and an evergreen crown in which several tall, lighted candles are set. Then she takes coffee and 'Lucia' buns to her family. Her brothers and sisters accompany her, the boys dressed as stars in long white shirts and pointed hats.

"That is what happens today; but of course, the festival of St. Lucia is probably older than the Christian story. It used to be the custom in Sweden to elect a Lucia, Queen of Brides. She would visit local homes and farms with trays of food, and the crown of candles on her head. She also visited the animals in their sheds, to bring light and good fortune to animals and people alike. Nowadays, many of your people forget to bless the animals, little one. They would do well to remember. But now it is time for us to make another journey. Hold my paw and close your eyes."

HANUKKAH

"CAN I OPEN MY EYES YET?" asked the girl.

"In a moment," replied the bear. "But you must learn to be patient! First, listen. What can you hear?"

"I can hear a voice…it sounds like the deep voice of a man. I can't understand the words, but it sounds as though he is praying. Can I look now?"

"Look with the eye of your mind and listen for a little longer. Do you remember what I told you about the sun? Many people use the sun to measure time, and they have a solar calendar; but others use the moon as their guide. The Jewish calendar is a lunar calendar, and every month begins with a new moon. The festival of Hanukkah, or the Festival of Lights, is celebrated on the twenty-fifth day of Kislev, which falls in the month you call December."

"Hanukkah. That's an interesting word," said the girl, and she turned it around in her mind.

"Yes. It means 'dedication.' At the festival of Hanukkah, Jewish people celebrate the rededication of the temple in Jerusalem after it had been defiled by a Greek leader, Antiochus, who tried to make all Jews give up their religion. You can open your eyes now. Look! Do you see the lights burning in that window? How many can you count?"

"I can count nine candles, but only five of them are alight."

"That is because tonight is the fourth night of Hanukkah. Jewish people who celebrate this festival light one candle more on each successive night until there are eight lights shining on their Hanukkah candlestick, or menorah. The ninth candle, the tall one in the middle, is called the servant light, or 'samash,' and it is used to light the others.

"The candles are lit as soon as the first three stars appear in the evening sky, and they must burn for half an hour each night. The man you see standing near the menorah is the father. It is he whom you heard reciting the prayer."

"And there is a delicious smell coming from inside the house!" exclaimed the girl.

"There certainly is! Delicious foods are served at Hanukkah, especially latkes, which are a kind of potato cake, and doughnuts. Both of these foods are cooked in oil; you will soon learn why the oil is important! Many games are played too, including the spinning of the dreidel or square top. It has the Hebrew letters N, G, H and Sh written on its four sides. Each child lays down some sweets or coins and takes turns to spin the dreidel: if the top lands on N, nothing is gained. On G, the spinner gets all the sweets. On H, half the sweets. On Sh, the child has to put another sweet on the pile. Together, the letters on the dreidel spell out 'nes gadol hayah sham,' which is Hebrew for 'a great miracle happened here.' Now listen carefully, and I shall tell you how that miracle came about."

A GREAT MIRACLE HAPPENED HERE

~THE STORY OF HANUKKAH~

Once upon a time in the Holy Land, the Jewish people found themselves at war with a man called Antiochus. He was a Syrian Greek, and he had decided to conquer the Holy Land. He did not like the way the Jews had their own religion and laws, so he brought his great armies to Jerusalem. His men broke down the city walls and forced their way into the Temple.

To the people's horror, he stole the treasures of the Temple and placed a statue of his own god, Zeus, on the altar there. To insult the Jewish laws, which forbid the eating of pork, Antiochus even sacrificed a pig at the altar and sprinkled its unclean blood all around the sanctuary, which was the holiest part of the Temple.

Antiochus then forbade the Jews to practice their religion and, to make sure, he ransacked the houses of prayer — the synagogues — and burned the houses of study. So great were his armies that it was impossible to stop him.

But, in a little village not far from Jerusalem, there was an old priest called Mattathias, who had five sons. One of Antiochus's men, Apelles, came to their village and set up an altar to the Greek gods. Then he ordered the villagers to make offerings to the gods. Mattathias gathered his sons about him and said, "I am an old man and I shall not live much longer, but of this I am sure. I shall never betray my faith and worship these Greek gods. Our people are carried off into slavery or run away into exile, our priests and scholars are killed, our Temple is polluted. I say that we should rebel."

His five sons swore that they would defend their faith. They followed their father into the street. Mattathias went up to Apelles and killed him, shouting to the rest of the village, "Take up arms, all who are on the side of the Living God, and follow me."

For one full year, Mattathias and his sons led the rebellion against the
Greeks. Their bravery inspired many others, and soon the Jews had an
army of their own hiding in the hills. Of all their warriors, the bravest
and strongest was a man called Judas. When Mattathias died, Judas took
his place. Because his family had been so committed to the cause of Jewish
freedom, Mattathias and his sons were known as the Maccabees: the
hammers of God.

Inspired by the sacred struggle of his people, Judas won many great
victories against Antiochus and his followers. More and more rebels
came to their side. Then there arose a great opportunity. A messenger
came to Judas and told him, "Antiochus is short of money to pay his
huge army. He is traveling into Persia to beg the help of rich money-
lenders. He has left his generals in charge of his main encampment near
the city of Emmaus."

Judas prepared his men for battle, for, with Antiochus gone, this was a chance not to be missed. After they had prayed and fasted for strength, Judas called them together.

"All of you who are afraid of the coming battle, all of you who are planting your vineyards, all of you who are newly married: go from the field! In this battle, only those who are single-minded about restoring the freedom of our people and our faith should fight with us. Do not be afraid of the great numbers of our enemies, but call upon God to aid us."

Judas received word from his spies that the Greek army had split into two, and that one half was coming toward them. He made his men abandon their camp, but leave the camp-fires burning to make the Greeks think they were still there. Then Judas and his men rode on to the main Greek encampment, where they slew the followers of Antiochus. The other half of the Greek army, realizing they had been tricked, returned to

the main camp. But seeing that Judas had killed all their fellow soldiers, they fled at once in terror, leaving Judas master of the field.

Now Judas led his men into the city of Jerusalem. It was a sorry sight. But when he reached the Temple, tears of anger and grief brimmed in his eyes. The beautiful Temple, the House of God, was ruined and defiled by the Greeks. Judas brought together the priests who had remained in hiding and they set about restoring the Temple.

When the new altar had been set up and a new menorah had been made, it was time to rededicate the Temple. But when the lights of the menorah were about to be kindled, the priests could find only one small flask of holy oil. It could not possibly last for more than a day. Then a great miracle happened. The lights did not go out at the end of the first day. Somehow the oil lasted for eight days and eight nights, until fresh supplies of pure oil were brought in.

To celebrate this miracle, Judas Maccabee and his brothers proclaimed that each year, on the twenty-fifth day of Kislev, the Jewish people would remember this time. A new festival called Hanukkah would be held for eight days. People were to light a new light every evening, and sing songs of praise to celebrate the Jewish people's newfound freedom.

SOLSTICE CUSTOMS

"SOME PEOPLE SAY that winter is a time of death, but it is really a time of sleeping. The seeds that are deep in the ground are waiting for the rain and sun of spring to awaken them. Some animals, like us bears, are hibernating, while others move to warmer climates. In the woods and forests, some trees have shed their leaves, but others retain theirs all year round. These evergreen trees take on a special importance to you humans in the winter months.

"Long ago, before the arrival of Christianity as well as after, the people of Europe honored the Green Lord and Lady, the god and goddess who symbolized the constant renewal of life. In many homes, the Green Lord and Lady have been forgotten, and not many humans see them now, though the animals know they are there. The Green Lord and Lady are the guardians of the deep places where animals can come and be at peace with each other, unharmed by humans. On the day of the midwinter solstice, the shortest day of the year, they make merry in the forest clearings.

"Even if they do not realize it, people pay tribute to the Green Lord and Lady when they decorate their homes for Christmas with wreaths, and with holly and ivy. Another plant which people hang up in their homes, usually over entrance-ways, is mistletoe. With its finger-shaped leaves and white berries, it reminds us of the skillful druids, the holy people of the Celtic tribes who cut mistletoe growing high in trees with a golden sickle and caught it in a white cloth. Mistletoe brings fertility, it is believed, and it is the custom to kiss under the mistletoe bough hung up in the hall.

"The midwinter solstice falls on December 21. But we are moving ahead of ourselves. Hold my paw and close your eyes."

"This is a very colorful place!"

"It certainly is. This is Mexico City, and the family you can see knocking on that door across the street are following an old custom called 'las posadas'. From December 16 until Christmas Eve, Mexicans remember the hardships of Mary and Joseph as they looked for somewhere to shelter in Bethlehem. Families take turns to visit each other's houses carrying lighted candles. They knock to be let in, but the people inside refuse them at first. Finally they are allowed to enter, and everyone kneels around the crib to sing carols.

"Afterward, children try to win the piñata, which is a container in the shape of an animal, stuffed with sweets and toys. The piñata is hung up and each child, blindfolded, tries to break it open with a stick. When it finally bursts, all the sweets and toys spill out and there is a great scramble to pick them up. But remember! The real gift of the midwinter season is sweeter than this. Now, hold my paw and close your eyes."

THE CHRISTINGLE

"WHAT A BEAUTIFUL CANDLE!"

"Yes, it is very beautiful. This is a Christingle. We are in an old Scandinavian church, high in the mountains, and the children you can see have come to a Christingle service. Do you recognize the fruit that supports the candle?"

"It looks like an orange."

"That's right. The orange represents the world. What else do you see?"

"There is a red ribbon around the orange."

"The red ribbon represents the blood of Christ."

"And what are the four sticks?"

"The four sticks are the four seasons. Now, what do you think the candle represents?"

"Is it the light that is inside each of us?"

"I suppose it is! And for Christians, it is the light of Christ. So now it is time for you to hear the Christmas story. Like all good stories, it has changed throughout the centuries. The story I like most comes from the teachings of St. James, and from an old Irish legend. Listen carefully!"

The BLESSING
of the ANGELS

~THE STORY OF CHRISTMAS~

For hundreds of years, the Jews had waited for God's Messiah, whose coming had been foreseen by their prophets and holy men. No one expected this Messiah to arrive in a simple place; they thought that he would be born into a rich and important family. But that is not what happened.

One year the Romans, who were then ruling Judea, held a census. This meant that everyone had to go to their hometown to be registered. Now, there lived in Judea a man called Joseph and his wife, Mary, who was soon to give birth to a child. Joseph knew that Mary's baby was very special, because an angel had appeared to him in a dream, and told him, "Mary will have a child of the Holy Spirit of God. He will be called Jesus, the Anointed One, the Christ, and he will save the people from all error."

When he heard about the census, Joseph was dismayed. He knew that the journey to his hometown of Bethlehem would be very uncomfortable for Mary, because her baby would be born very soon. Still, the couple had

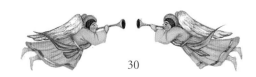

no choice. So they took their donkey to carry Mary, and began the long journey.

It was evening as the couple came to the outskirts of Bethlehem. Suddenly Mary was gripped with the pains of labor and cried out, "Joseph, find somewhere for me to lie down and go and fetch me a midwife, I beg you."

Joseph found a cave where animals were tethered and laid Mary gently down upon the fragrant straw. Then he hurried into the village to find the midwife. A kindly innkeeper directed him to a woman called Salome. "Please come and attend my wife!" Joseph begged. "She is about to give birth to the Son of the Highest and she needs your skills."

Salome looked at him, amazed. "Do you expect me to believe such a story?" she exclaimed. "Has the journey here quite addled your wits, old man?" Still, she followed him. As they approached the cave, she saw that there was a bright, holy cloud overshadowing it and realized she had spoken too harshly. "Wait here, good man, and forgive my foolish words. I will go at once to your wife." And she hurried inside.

Joseph walked about the village, anxiously waiting for the birth. As he waited, time stood still. When he looked up in the air, he saw that the birds were poised there without motion. When he looked down the street, he saw workmen at their dinner tables: one man had his hand in the dish and another had food raised to his mouth. Neither of them moved. The shepherds on the hill had their crooks raised to herd the sheep, but not a breath of wind stirred their motionless figures. The goats at the ford had their mouths to the water, but neither goat nor water stirred. Then, as if by an unseen signal, everything started to move again. And, in that moment, Joseph knew that the child had been born. He hurried into the cave and found Mary with her son at her breast. With the midwife, he fell to his knees to adore the baby who was also the Son of God.

The Holy Family stayed in the cave, visited only by shepherds who had heard angels singing while they guarded their sheep.

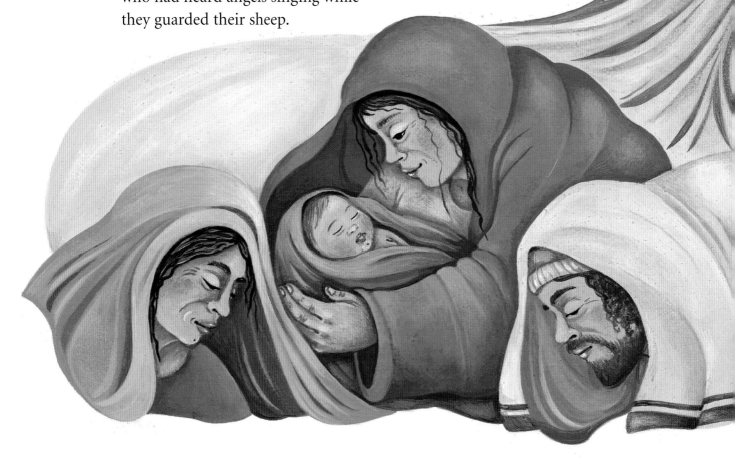

Far away from the quiet village of Bethlehem, three wise kings from the East made their way to King Herod in Jerusalem. They asked him about the newborn king whose birth had been foretold by the arrival of a new star in the skies. Herod's advisers told him that such a star heralded the birth of the Christ, the Anointed One, who would put everything right in the world. Christ was to be born in the village of Bethlehem.

And so it was to Bethlehem that the three wise kings traveled. The star that they were following stopped over the cave where Mary and Jesus were resting. The kings presented rich gifts of shining gold, fragrant frankincense and pungent-smelling myrrh.

Meanwhile, King Herod began to feel disturbed by the kings' visit. He feared this newborn child who would be a greater king than himself. So he gave an order that all boys under the age of two should be murdered, and sent out his soldiers to round up all such children.

When Mary heard about this dreadful order, she wrapped Jesus in swaddling clothes to still his little limbs and hid him in the manger where the oxen and asses thrust their soft mouths into the hay. Their breath would hide him from the soldiers, and the beasts would do him no harm.

In due course, the soldiers came to the village of Bethlehem to put all the baby boys to death. Once again, Joseph dreamed of the angel. This time the angel told him that he and Mary would be safer if they went into Egypt, instead of going home, until the bloodshed was over. So Mary sent for Salome, the midwife, and asked her to help them escape. "Leave it to me," said Salome. To Joseph she said, "Make ready to leave as soon as I give the word."

At dusk Joseph helped Mary with the baby onto the donkey, put his bundle onto his shoulders and, guided by Salome, they skirted the village. But as they approached the road to safety, some rowdy soldiers came by. They had spent all day killing little children and their hearts were sore with the dreadful deed. Despite having drunk large amounts of wine to try to forget what they had done, they were still mindful of the task in hand.

Salome gestured the Holy Family back into the shadows and quickly kindled a flame. Under her cloak she had been carrying a crown of candles and now she lit them up and put the crown on her head. She sang loudly and danced to attract the soldiers' attention. In the darkness the flaming crown drew all eyes, dazzling the onlookers, hiding the Holy Family in the shadows.

The soldiers roared out delightedly at the sight of Salome capering about in the street and they followed her back into the village, just as she had intended them to. As soon as their drunken roars drew away into the distance, Joseph led the donkey away from the danger of Judea into the safety of Egypt.

And there the Holy Family stayed until they heard of the death of King Herod a few years later. Then, with pride and joy, Joseph led his dear wife, Mary, and her little son back to Judea, and to a story that is even more wondrous than this.

CHRISTMAS CUSTOMS

"WAS JESUS REALLY the Christ, and the Son of the Most High?"

"Many people believe that he was. And every year they celebrate his birth on December 25. No one knows the exact date that he was born, but early Christians chose this day because it was already a time of midwinter celebration, when people prayed that the sun would return. The calendar has changed entirely since then. The shortest day falls on December 21, but Christmas is still celebrated on December 25, except in the Orthodox Church, where it is celebrated on January 6.

"The story of Jesus's birth is important to Christians because it tells of God coming into the world in the person of Jesus. Jesus was both Man and God. When he grew up, he healed many people and taught them how to awaken the light of God inside themselves. 'I am the light of the world,' he said. 'Whoever follows me will have the light of life and will never walk in darkness.'

"This is why the lighting of candles plays an important part in Christmas celebrations. In the four weeks before Christmas, which are called Advent, some families put up Advent wreaths. An Advent wreath has four candles, one for each Sunday, and a fifth in the center for Christmas Day. And on Christmas Eve, many churches hold a candlelit service at midnight."

"What do the children do?"

"In some families, the children hang up Christmas stockings. In the olden days, Christmas stockings would contain an orange for the sun, a silver coin for the moon, and a lump of coal for the fire. Nowadays they are usually filled with gifts."

"Do stockings contain the best gift of all?"

"Pay attention and you will find out. Now, hold my paw and close your eyes. We are going to a village in the mountains of Austria, to hear an old Christmas legend."

SCHNITZLE, SCHNOTZLE
and SCHNOOTZLE

~A STORY FOR CHRISTMAS NIGHT~

Many Christmases ago, there lived a very poor cobbler and his three sons, Fritzel, Franzel and Hansel. His wife had died some years before and he tried hard to feed his family. In good times, when the cobbler mended a farmer's Sunday shoes, they would drink good goat's milk. If he mended the baker's wife's shoes, they would eat a stick of crusty bread. If the butcher's shoes were to be mended, then they would have a rich stew in a big pot, with vegetables, noodles and herbs to make it tasty and filling.

And when they sat down to their stew, the cobbler would laugh and clap his hands together and proclaim, "Well, boys! Today we have a good…Schnitzle, Schnotzle and Schnootzle." And the boys would laugh with glee as their father ladled out the stew into each brimming bowl. They didn't care what their father called it, so long as there was more of the lovely stew to eat.

Those were the rich times, when they had full bellies. But there came

a year that was worse than all other years. War came to their land. People had so little money that they went with unmended shoes, and the cobbler had nothing much to feed the children. In the summertime and fall, they could manage to live off the land, for there were grain, berries and roots. But as December arrived, the land was stripped bare and the winter brought nothing but hunger.

All the little boys were wondering what kind of Christmas they would have that year. They very much hoped that Father would come home with something good to eat and sit down, as ever, and cry out, "Now, this being Christmas, we have a nice…" and the boys would shout the response, "Schnitzle, Schnotzle and Schnootzle!" But it had been a long time since the butcher's shoes had been mended.

Christmas Eve came and the boys huddled around a small fire as their father arrived home. "I've not mended any shoes today, boys, but I've just heard that the inn is packed with soldiers. Marching men always need a little help from the cobbler, so I'm going there now and you'll see what I'll come back with — a little…"

"Schnitzle, Schnotzle and Schnootzle," the boys chorused, rather hollowly, as they had eaten nothing since breakfast time.

The cobbler piled on his warmest clothes and put his tools together in a rucksack. "Now keep the fire going, bolt the door after me, pull the quilt over you, and don't let anyone in!" And out he went into the howling wind of the cold Christmas night. Fritzel stared out of the window and tried not to think of how hopeful and hungry his dear father looked as he tramped down the mountainside to the valley below.

Then the three boys did as they were told and rolled themselves under the quilt and listened to the quiet sizzling of the fire. After a while, they heard a knocking at the door. "Let me in! Let me in!" came a high, squeaky voice. Fritzel ran to the door and was about to lift the bolt.

"Remember what Father said!" cried Franzel. Hansel just peered out from a fold in the quilt, too frightened to move.

Fritzel looked through a crack in the door and saw, standing in the snow, a very small man who was no bigger than little Hansel. His teeth were chattering and he was all a-shiver, from head to toe.

"Don't open it," hissed Franzel.

"I must," said Fritzel. "The little man is freezing." And he lifted the bolt and in stalked the strangest little man they had ever seen. Under his high peaked hat they saw a large red face with a broad nose, and under that a long red beard.

"You've kept me waiting a long time! Hogging all the fire and food to yourselves, I see!" said the stranger in his funny high voice, which didn't seem to belong to his short, stumpy body. He looked meaningfully at the poor fire, which was nearly out, and at the empty table and shelves where no food was stored.

"Well, the least you can do for me is to warm me up!" announced the little man. And with that, he climbed into the big straw bed. Franzel and Hansel drew back in amazement. Fritzel tried to explain that it wasn't for lack of welcome that they couldn't be more hospitable to the stranger, only that they had no firewood and no food left.

"Well, roll over! Can't you see I have no room to sleep?" And he grabbed one half of the quilt and wrapped himself in it.

Fritzel said as politely as he could, "Sir, these little ones must be allowed to sleep too. There's room enough for all, if you will let them be," and he began to climb into bed himself, for it was getting colder by the minute as the meager fire began to die down.

The little man bounced and rolled, shouting, "More quilt! More room! I'm very cold and very hungry," and he poked little Hansel angrily.

"Be gentle, sir!" rebuked Fritzel, trying to be polite. "We promise that as soon as our father returns with some food, you will share it."

"Promises are all very good," grumbled their visitor. "If you mean so well, then you must give me your place in bed," and he kicked Fritzel out of the bed. "If you want to keep warm, then why don't you turn some cartwheels?"

Fritzel was propelled from the bed so suddenly that he found himself turning cartwheels across the room. As he turned, so — plop, plop, plop! — things came falling out of his pockets. Franzel and Hansel began to cry out in astonishment. Every time their brother turned a cartwheel, golden oranges fell from his pockets, along with sugar sweets in gold and silver paper.

"You as well!" said the little man, pushing Franzel out of bed. "Go and spin some cartwheels like your brother!"

And soon Franzel found himself rolling about the room and — plop, plop, plop! — out of his pockets came Christmas buns and gingerbread with icing, and cookies all covered with almonds and raisins.

"Now I shall sleep soundly," said the visitor, pushing little Hansel out of bed. "Off you go! Spin a few cartwheels, that's the thing!" Then Hansel

soon found himself turning cartwheels too — something he had never done before — all about the floor. And out of his pockets — clang, clang, clankerty-clang! — came great fat golden coins, pouring onto the floor like golden hail.

The boys could not believe their good fortune. After they had danced about the room, singing for joy, Fritzel turned to the bed to say, "Now we can offer you better Christmas cheer…" when he saw that the bed was rumpled but quite, quite empty. The visitor had vanished.

The boys gathered up their treasure: they set the shining oranges into bowls, put the buns and cookies on the best platter, and poured the gold into as many dishes as they possessed. Then in walked their father, with bread, milk, noodles and meat. The soldiers had paid him in money and he had bought all that they needed.

But his eyes nearly came out of his head in astonishment when he saw what was upon the table. The boys' explanations tumbled over each other as they tried to tell the story of what had happened. When the cobbler pieced together their account, he shook his head wisely and knowingly. "So it's true what my grandfather used to say."

"What's that, Father?" asked the boys.

"Well, he used to say that King Laurin, the leader of all the goblins in the High Tyrol, used to come to one home every Christmas. He would play his tricks and share his mighty treasure."

Franzel and Fritzel exchanged wondering glances as their father prepared the meal. Fancy! A goblin king in their own home!

"Well, I don't think he was very nice!" cried Hansel. "He poked me and kicked us out of our own bed."

"He didn't hurt us really, Father," said Fritzel. "It was just his way."

"He was pretending to be fierce, but he wasn't really frightening," agreed Franzel.

As they sat down at the table, the rich savory smell of stew wafted up and filled the room, joining the sweet odor of sugary cookies, spicy gingerbread and oranges. The cobbler looked gleefully around the table, "And what do we have to eat here? Some…"

"Schnitzle, Schnotzle and Schnootzle!" chorused the boys in one big shout.

THE *T*WELVE DAYS OF CHRISTMAS

"THOSE BOYS RECEIVED WONDERFUL GIFTS, didn't they?" said the girl.

"Oh yes. And now it is time for you to learn a little more about gifts. Hold my paw and close your eyes; we are going to England now, to an old village where some of the old ways are still alive."

"What a curious building this is! All of the walls are made of trees. And…are they alive?"

"They are very much alive, and so is everyone who has gathered here. For this is the hall of story, and the hall of song, ruled over by the king and queen of time and eternity. Listen! It is time for the song."

On the first day of Christmas
My true love gave to me
A partridge in a pear tree.

On the second day of Christmas
My true love gave to me
Two turtle-doves
And a partridge in a pear tree.

On the third day of Christmas
My true love gave to me
Three French hens,
Two turtle-doves
And a partridge in a pear tree.

On the fourth day of Christmas
My true love gave to me
Four colly birds...
And a partridge in a pear tree.

On the fifth day of Christmas
My true love gave to me
Five gold rings...
And a partridge in a pear tree.

On the sixth day of Christmas
My true love gave to me
Six geese a-laying...
And a partridge in a pear tree.

On the seventh day of Christmas
My true love gave to me
Seven swans a-swimming...
And a partridge in a pear tree.

On the eighth day of Christmas
My true love gave to me
Eight maids a-milking...
And a partridge in a pear tree.

On the ninth day of Christmas
My true love gave to me
Nine drummers drumming...
And a partridge in a pear tree.

On the tenth day of Christmas
My true love gave to me
Ten pipers piping...
And a partridge in a pear tree.

On the eleventh day of Christmas
My true love gave to me
Eleven ladies dancing...
And a partridge in a pear tree.

On the twelfth day of Christmas
My true love gave to me
Twelve lords a-leaping...
And a partridge in a pear tree.

"What a marvelous song! But what does it all mean?"

"Have you learned how to count?"

"Yes..."

"Are you good at counting?"

"I think so..."

"Well, when I have finished my stories, count all the gifts that the singer receives from her true love and tell me what the number is. Can you do that?"

"I'll try."

"And now, shall we join the dance?"

THE CHRISTMAS CRIB

"I AM SO DIZZY I CAN HARDLY STAND! Oh! Everything has changed! Are we in a cave? Is this Bethlehem?"

"We are not in Bethlehem, we are in Greccio, high in the hills of Umbria, in Italy. This is the home of St. Francis."

"Which one is he?"

"He is the monk you see kneeling before the crib. The shepherds are local men whom he saw a few nights ago, asleep on the hill. He was so moved by this sight that he decided to re-create the birth of Jesus with local people. So here you see real people as Mary and Joseph too, and even a living baby as Jesus."

"They all look so peaceful, even the animals!"

"This is a holy place, child. Yes, everyone is at peace: animals with people, and people with their God. In Italian this scene is called a 'presepio.'"

"Oh dear, another word I don't understand."

"In English, we would say 'crib.' Since the time of St. Francis, in the fifteenth century, it has become customary in many Christian countries to recreate the scene of the Nativity. Some of them are quite small models, but in the churches of Italy, people still take great pride in their cribs. During the Christmas holiday, many families visit the churches in their neighborhood to admire the different cribs and offer a prayer to the newborn baby Jesus and his parents."

"It is so magical here! Do we have to leave?"

"It is time, little one, but remember that you can take what you have seen with you in your heart. Now, hold my paw and close your eyes."

NEW YEAR CUSTOMS

"I CAN HEAR LOTS OF SINGING AND SHOUTING! What's happening? Now there are bells ringing out..."

"Yes, and we can sing too! Open your eyes! This is Princes Street in Edinburgh, the capital city of Scotland. The Scots call the New Year 'Hogmanay.' Let's sing with them!"

Here's a health to them that's away,
Here's a health to them that's away.
Here's a health to them that were here a while
And cannot be here today.

"Now, let's follow that man and see what happens next!"

"What is he carrying?"

"He has a lump of coal and he is 'first-footing.' In Scotland, the first person to knock on your door after midnight on New Year's Eve cannot be turned away. To bring the blessing of warmth to the household, the man is carrying a lump of coal. Of course, he will stay for a while and be offered a warming tot of whisky! But we cannot stay with him. We have another journey to make. Hold my paw and close your eyes."

"There is laughter and singing here too, but the voices sound quite different!"

"That is because we are on the other side of the Atlantic Ocean, in North Carolina in America. It is New Year's Day, and the women are busy preparing Hopping John."

"Hopping John? Who is he? What are they preparing him for?"

"He is not a person, little one, he is a kind of food! All over the southern United States, people eat plates of black-eyed peas and rice on New Year's Day. You are supposed to have as much money in the coming year as the amount of peas you eat. In other countries, people eat lentils for the same reason."

"Does it work?"

"I don't know, child. How should I? We bears have no use for money! And now that we are in the United States, will you join me for a Kwanzaa party?"

"Yes, please! Where do we have to go?"

"Hold my paw and close your eyes!"

KWANZAA

"I SEE A LOT OF PEOPLE gathered around the table. Who are they and what are they doing?"

"They're African Americans who have all come together to celebrate Kwanzaa. It's a new festival, but it remembers many ancient things. This family has gathered to give thanks for all that is good in the universe."

"What are the seven candles for?"

"The candles represent unity, self-determination, work and responsibility, sharing, purpose, creativity and faith. Everyone here is remembering these important things and promising to make space for them in their lives."

"Why are they pouring out the drink in the cup?"

"That's the cup of unity. By passing the cup around and sharing it together, by pouring it out upon the ground, they are remembering with love all of their ancestors."

"Who are their ancestors?"

"All the many family members who are no longer living but whose long struggle from slavery to freedom makes celebrating Kwanzaa possible today. People in this country celebrate Kwanzaa from December 26 to January 1. This is December 31, and African Americans all over North America are gathering for a banquet of African food and to exchange gifts."

"What kind of soup is that on the table?"

"It's a special African soup and different families make it in different ways. It usually has a few ingredients in common: salt, sauce, spice, onion, pepper and dripping. Now, everyone likes their soup one way or another. Some like it salty, some prefer a good sauce, others like it spicy, most like onion and a few like their soup hot and peppery. But who likes the dripping that greases the pot? You don't? Well, listen to this story."

A RECIPE *for* BETTER TIMES

~A STORY FOR NEW YEAR'S EVE~

Once upon a time there were six sisters called Salt, Sauce, Spice, Onion, Pepper and Dripping. One day they heard tell of a handsome young man and they decided to see if he wanted one of them as a wife.

They all set off together, but soon the other sisters were telling Dripping to stand away from them because she stank. Ashamed, she crept off but followed behind them at a distance.

The sisters came across an old woman bathing in a stream. Dripping crept forward and said to her sisters, "It would be respectful to our elders to scrub her back for her."

"Heaven preserve me from touching that ugly old woman!" said Sauce and the others agreed. Let someone else help her! And the sisters continued on their way. All except Dripping, who greeted the old woman from the reeds. "Can I help you, grandmother?" she called.

"Certainly, young woman! Now, tell me, where are you going?"

Dripping said, shyly, "Well, I heard about a handsome boy who lives nearby and I wondered..."

"You wondered whether he might want a wife, I expect?" said the old woman, sagely.

Dripping nodded.

"But do you know his name?"

Dripping shook her head.

The old woman drew her garment around her and whispered, "His name is Daskandarini, but you mustn't tell your sisters."

Dripping thanked her and set off on her way.

Meanwhile the other girls had reached the place where the handsome young man lived. They hung back and giggled together, agreeing that they would each go in and speak to him one at a time.

Salt stooped to enter his hut, but his voice called, "Who is at my door?"

"It's me, Salt."

"Well, Salt, do you have the grit to tell me my name?"

But Salt didn't know it and she was sent away.

Sauce came next. "Who are you?" asked the voice.

"I'm Sauce."

"Well, Sauce, are you saucy enough to tell me my name?"

But she wasn't and was sent away.

Then Spice tried. "Who is it?" cried the young man.

"It's Spice."

"Well, Spice, are you sharp enough to know my name?"

But she wasn't and she was sent away.

Then Onion tried. "Who is there?" cried the voice.

"I'm Onion."

"Well, Onion, can you stop crying long enough to tell me my name?"
But she didn't know it, and soon enough she was sent away crying.
Then Pepper tried. "Who's there?" asked the young man.
"It's me, Pepper."
"Well, Pepper, are you hot enough to know my name?"
But she wasn't and she was sent away too.

The five sisters huddled together, angry and upset at their failure.
Then they saw Dripping, and said to her, "Well, are you going in?"

"I don't know," said Dripping. "How can I think of it when such lovely girls as you have been driven away? He's bound to send away one who stinks of dripping."

"Go on and try," urged the sisters, who wanted to see how badly she would fail.

Dripping stooped to enter. "Who is there?" cried the voice.

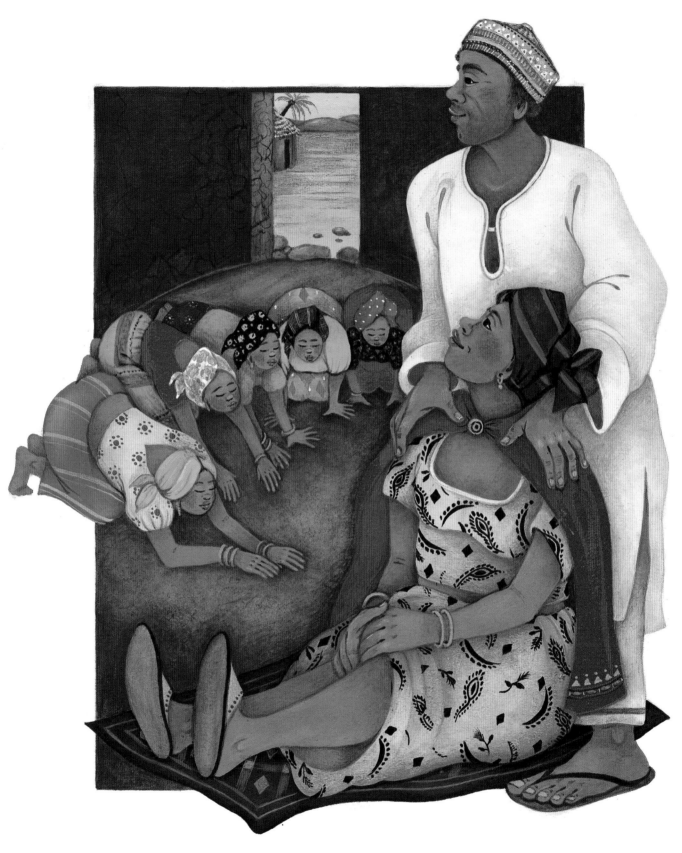

"It's me, Dripping."

"Well, Dripping, are you able to cut the butter and tell me what my name is?"

"Certainly — you are Daskandarini!" she declared.

Daskandarini came to the door and invited her inside. He spread a rug for her to sit upon. He wrapped a rich garment about her shoulders and brought slippers of gold for her feet. "It is you, Dripping, who will be my wife," he announced.

The five sisters, who had been listening outside with their ears pressed to the wall of the hut, were astounded. They looked at one another and made a decision.

One by one, they fell upon their knees before Dripping.

"Let me mash food for you," said Salt.

"Let me sweep for you," begged Sauce.

"Let me draw water for you," offered Spice.

"Let me mix the ingredients of your soup," said Onion.

"Let me stir your food for you," begged Pepper.

And at once Dripping gained five obedient servants.

Now, it's from such ordinary things as this that our soup is made. When they are cooked together, they make something good to eat. And just as ordinary objects can be transformed into something extraordinary, so if you see a poor man or woman, you shouldn't despise them. Who knows, one day they may be better than you.

The soup is made! Happy Kwanzaa, everyone!

TWELFTH NIGHT CUSTOMS

"Now, child, the midwinter holiday is almost over. This is Twelfth Night, the last of the twelve days of Christmas. Do you remember the song we heard when we were in the hall of story?"

"Yes, and I have counted all of the gifts."

"And what number did you reach?"

"Three hundred and sixty-four. But what is so special about that? And what is the best gift, anyway?"

"Patience, patience. How many days are there in the year?"

"Easy. Three hundred and sixty-five. Did the person who made up the song make a mistake?"

"He did not, whoever he or she was. The queen receives three hundred and sixty-four gifts from the king. But the best gift of all, the gift that enables life to continue, the gift that closes the old year and gives birth to the new, is the gift of true love. So the true love the king has for the queen makes life possible."

"What about other people?"

"There is a king in all of us, and a queen too. In this song, and in many old traditions, the king symbolizes the sun, and the queen symbolizes the moon. Now, you already know about the importance of light in this world. The sun and the moon are the two great lights, and they also represent the principles of male and female. You may not always see or sense it, but you are part of a huge cosmic dance, and what makes that dance happen is the movement between male and female. It has always been so and it will always be. Look up above you!"

On the ceiling of the cave, the girl saw the starry constellations wheeling around. She found a pattern of stars that made the shape of a big bear.

"Is that you over there — the big one with the seven stars?"

"That's me dancing in the sky," said the bear.

"You have your tail in the air and you're twirling around and around!"

"Bears always stay close to home," said the bear. "I do my dance so that everyone will know where to find north."

"Is north very important, then?"

"It is where the winter comes from. As long as I am dancing around and around, the winter will change to spring, and spring to summer, and summer to fall..."

"And fall to winter again?" said the girl.

"Yes," said the bear.

"May I have another story?" asked the girl

"Of course you may. This is a story about the Epiphany, for Twelfth Night is also the day when the three wise kings visited the baby Jesus and gave him their gifts. In Russia and Greece, this is also the day when people celebrate Christmas. So let's have another Russian story!"

BABOUSHKA

~A STORY FOR TWELFTH NIGHT~

Many years ago, in the land of Russia, there lived a woman called Baboushka. Her house was the most beautifully kept in the whole village. From the brightly colored gables on her wooden roof, right down to her neat little garden, her house was a sight to behold.

Although she lived alone, Baboushka was forever washing and cleaning, baking and cooking, painting and gardening, as if she was expecting a special guest. Although she was past the age of motherhood, she especially loved children and she spent the long, cold winter months making fine little toys. Her hands were clever and strong, and her heart was pure and generous. Everyone in the village was very fond of her.

One evening, in the great expanse of the heavens, there appeared an enormous star with a trailing tail that moved across the sky. Everyone in the village was very excited about the new star, wondering what it could mean, but Baboushka merely smiled and shook her head. "Whatever it means, there is still the floor to be washed and the bread to be baked."

But the very next day, the meaning became plain. Over the hills beyond the village came a procession of strangers. They had come from very far off. In the procession were three mighty kings. There was bearded Caspar in his crown of gold, riding upon a high-stepping black horse. There was Melchior in his robes of white, fastened by a jewel shaped like a star, riding upon a fine camel. And there was Balthasar in his gold and red tunic, seated upon a magnificent white stallion. Each of the kings carried a special treasure.

The kings' servants rode down into the village to find lodgings. They sought out the headman and asked him which house was most fitting for their royal masters to sleep throughout that day, for the kings could travel only by night. The headman longed to invite these grand visitors to his own house, but he knew that it was too small and not fine enough. He had fourteen children and the house was often noisy and not always as clean as it might be. So he said to the servants, "Tell your royal masters to ask at the house with the colored gables."

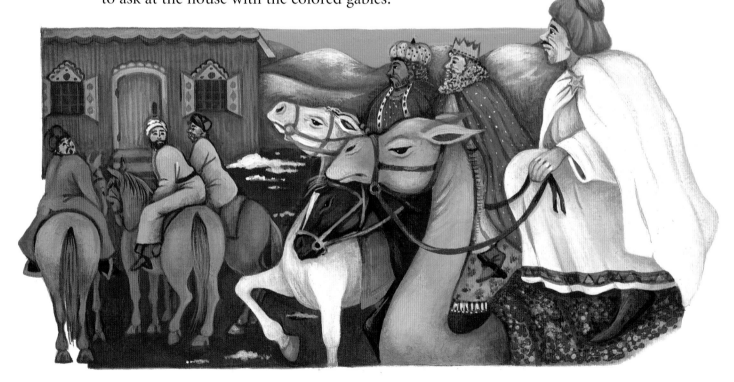

The kings dismounted outside Baboushka's house and knocked on the door. "Good woman," they said as she opened the door, "we need to rest here this day until the star once more appears in the sky. Do we have your leave to enter?"

Baboushka pressed her hands to her cheeks in astonishment, "Sirs, please come in. You are most welcome!"

Soon the three kings were sitting at her table and enjoying a meal of freshly cooked bread, beet soup, pickled herrings and vegetables, all washed down with birch-sap beer.

When they had eaten, Baboushka invited them to sit around her fire and tell her about their journey.

"We are following the star whose glory has been foretold by my people for many years," said Melchior, the firelight playing upon the starry jewel at his breast.

"Where does it lead?" asked Baboushka.

Caspar spoke from the depths of his beard. "We believe that the star will lead us to a king who is about to be born."

Balthasar's dark eyes flashed. "A king who is King of all the Universe. And we have brought him gifts."

Baboushka's eyes fell upon the precious things that the kings had brought with them, and her heart was strangely moved. If these great kings from countries far away thought it important enough to leave their kingdoms to find a humble newborn baby, then that child must be King indeed. If he were greater than they, then he was her King too.

"I wish I could bring him a present," she said, almost to herself.

"Then why don't you come with us?" suggested Balthasar.

Baboushka looked up, startled, not realizing that she had uttered her wish aloud.

While they slept soundly, Baboushka cleaned away the meal and tidied up the house. So many guests had left her with much more work than usual. Could she really leave home and travel with the three kings? What should she take as a gift? What things would she need for the journey?

At twilight, she wakened the sleeping kings, who made ready to leave. Balthasar stretched out his hand to include her in their procession. "Are you coming, Baboushka?"

"I have to find a gift. There is so much to get ready. I must tidy the house before I go. I will catch up with you."

The kings went on their way, following the star.

When she looked up and saw the star with her own eyes, Baboushka knew that she really had to go. She rushed back into the house and began to look through her store of gifts. There were wooden animals, carved and painted; there were birch-bark boxes filled with ribbons, polished stones and sweets; there were nesting dolls that sat inside each other; there were whistles made of reeds. Which would be good enough for a newborn king?

Baboushka simply could not decide which was best, so she packed all of them in a big basket. She could make her decision as she traveled, or else create something lovely along the way. By the time she had found her knife and paints, her scissors and threads, and packed them away with her own few things for the journey, she heard the sound of the rooster crowing that dawn was coming. She gave a great big yawn. How tired she was! She had been awake for a day and a night without sleep and now she fell into a deep slumber.

Baboushka woke up at twilight and rushed out with her basket, keeping the glorious star ever before her. In every village, she asked after the three kings and which way they had gone.

Wherever she asked, people would direct her on to the next village or town, pointing the way that the star was traveling. Baboushka trudged onward for days and months until she came to the royal palace of Jerusalem.

"At last! This must be where the newborn king will be found," Baboushka thought. She asked a guard outside the walls but he said, "Yes, the three kings came here but they soon departed, hurrying onward to a poor little place called Bethlehem."

Off she went at once. She arrived at twilight and saw how the great star seemed to be directly overhead. Her heart leaped. This must be the place! At the inn she asked the innkeeper, "Have the three kings been here?"

"Yes. They came to see the baby that was born in the stable here. But the kings have gone home now."

"And the baby?" asked Baboushka, with a trembling voice.

"Oh, the baby and his family went away as well — to Egypt, I think," said the innkeeper. Then, seeing her disappointment, he added, "I can show you the place where the baby was, if you like?"

Baboushka raised tear-filled eyes and followed him to the stable behind the inn. It was like a dimly lit cave inside. "This is where his mother laid him, in the straw of the manger," said the innkeeper. "Who would have thought that the Christ-child, Jesus, would be born in my stable?"

When Baboushka heard the baby's name, she fell on her knees.
Peering into the straw, she raised some of it to her face and kissed it. She
barely heard the innkeeper telling her about the visit of the shepherds
who had heard the message of angels, or about the presentation of gifts
by the three kings.

At the thought of the gift that she wanted to give the Christ-child,
Baboushka rose and thanked the innkeeper. "I'm going to find him, King
Jesus, and give him my gift," she said.

And, from that day to this, Baboushka journeys on with her basket of
toys, asking everywhere she goes for the newborn king. At every house,
especially at Christmas, she looks at the children asleep in their beds and
leaves a toy, just in case it might be the King of her heart.

CANDLEMAS CUSTOMS

"IT'S SO WARM AND COZY IN HERE! I wish we could stay in your den forever," whispered the girl.

"Some things are forever, and others are not. Your visit is nearly over, little one."

"Oh no! Has winter passed already? It seems as if I had only just arrived."

"Soon another light festival will be celebrated. The festival of Candlemas falls on February 2. For the Celts, this was the day when the first spark of light — the soul, if you like — entered the seeds that had been lying deep in the ground through the winter months. In many traditions, everything that lives and grows has a soul and a life force of its own, and deserves to be treated with respect. Even today, in many parts of the world, seeds are blessed before they are planted, and animals also receive blessings.

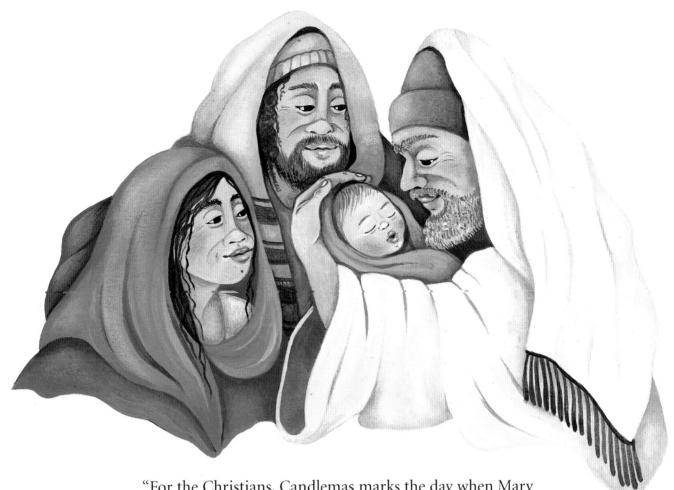

"For the Christians, Candlemas marks the day when Mary and Joseph took the infant Jesus to the Temple to be blessed by Simeon, a wise old man who knew when he took the baby in his arms that he held the Son of God. Candles are also blessed on this day, which is called Bear's Day in parts of central Europe."

"So is it a kind of birthday for you?"

"I suppose it is! Bear's Day is when we come out of our winter sleep. It is like Groundhog Day, when the groundhog emerges from its winter hibernation. Of course, we animals are not interested in the dates that humans have invented so we emerge when we sense that winter has passed. Today I have a feeling that spring is nearly here! So I think we should end with a story about a bear!"

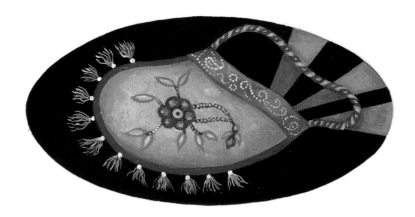

The BAG of WARMTH

~A STORY FOR THE RETURN OF THE SUN~

Long ago, before there were any people, there was a very long winter. The sun was hidden behind black clouds and the snow just kept falling and falling. After three years of this, the animals decided that they could not bear the darkness and cold any longer. So they called a meeting to discuss what they should do.

As the animals gathered in council, they agreed that it was lack of warmth that made them freeze with cold and starve for lack of food, but no one had any idea what they could do about it. Then the sharp-eyed wolf noticed that there were no bears at the council.

"Perhaps the bears know something which we don't. I wonder whether they are keeping all the warmth to themselves?" he said.

And it was decided that seven animals, the sharp-eyed wolf, the quick fox, the swift lynx, the nosy wolverine, the wise pike, the secret mouse and the strong dogfish, should go and seek the bears.

They knew that the bears lived in the upper world somewhere, but

how were they to find them? The wise pike made all the questing animals sit around the fire and chant for help. As they howled, barked, growled, snuffled, squeaked and bubbled in their own voices, the song rose up like a wind and shaped the smoke from their fire into a pathway. The animals rose up with it and passed through a hole in the sky.

In the upper world, they found a big lake with a hut built beside it. The animals went inside and saw two young bear-cubs huddled together by the fire.

"Where's your mother?" they asked the bear-cubs.

"Mother's gone hunting," the little bears replied.

The animals looked around the hut and saw that there were lots of bags hanging from poles. The swift lynx pointed at the bag nearest to him and asked, "What's in this bag?"

"Oh, Mother keeps the rain in that one," said the bear-cubs.

"What's in this one?" asked the secret mouse.

"Oh, that one is full of winds."

"And what's in this one?" asked the quick fox.

"That one has fog in it," said the little bears.

Nosy wolverine sniffed loudly at the bag nearest to him. "What about this one here?"

"Oh, we can't tell you about that. Mother keeps that one secret and we're not allowed to tell."

"You can tell us," said the secret mouse, sweetly encouraging. "We're your friends."

The little bears put their paws over their noses, remembering how hard their mother could cuff them. "Mother would beat us for telling you."

Swift lynx put his head on one side and said, "But how would she know what you'd done? We wouldn't tell her."

This confused the bear-cubs, but it seemed safe enough. "In that bag, she keeps the warmth," they said.

"Well, thank you kindly," said the sharp-eyed wolf, grinning.

The visitors went outside to have a council and to decide what to do.

"We need to distract the cubs so that we can steal the bag," said the wise pike.

"And we need to make sure that the bear won't run too fast after us once we've got the bag," said the secret mouse, who had shorter legs than the rest of them.

The secret mouse got up on to the quick fox's back, and the quick fox ran to where the bear's canoe was moored on the other side of the lake. Secret mouse immediately started to gnaw through part of the paddle. Then they waited until the bear herself came into view. Quick as a flash, swift lynx changed himself into a fat caribou calf.

The bear scented the caribou, and yelled for her children to come and help her. The cubs came tumbling out of the hut toward their mother. The caribou-lynx ran off at once and began to lead the bears deep into the forest. As soon as the bears had disappeared from sight, the other animals unhooked the bag of warmth and ran off with it.

Speedily doubling back to the lake, the caribou-lynx launched himself into the water and swam across to the other side. The mother bear began to follow in her canoe but her paddle broke into two pieces, and she pitched headlong into the lake. Down went the canoe.

The lynx changed swiftly back into his own form when he reached the other side of the lake. "Quickly now, let's run before she can follow us," he cried to the other animals.

The bag of warmth was very heavy, and the animals had to take it in turns to drag it back to the hole through which they had come. No matter how hard they tried, they could not pull it fast enough. Before they could reach the edge of the hole, they began to feel the bear's breath on the back of their necks. Then the silent dogfish, who had done nothing up until then, grabbed hold of the bag and whacked it through the hole with a shake of his strong tail. Down went the bag and with it went all the animals, tumbling through the path of smoke into their own world below.

As soon as they had regained their breath, they tore open the bag. Warmth rushed out and spread in all directions. The ice and snow began to melt, the black clouds began to dissolve and the sun came out once more. But the ice and snow melted so fast that they caused a terrible flood. The rivers flowed down to the seas so quickly that the seas began to rise all over the world.

The only thing left sticking out above the water was the tallest tree in the world. All the animals climbed into its mighty upper branches and called for help. Deep in the depths of the sea, a giant fish heard their cries and rose up to the surface. The fish swallowed up the flood waters, and it swelled to the size of a mountain. And there it remained as a great mountain forever afterwards.

The sun dried up the land, the trees and flowers began to bloom again, and summer was able to return. And that was how the animals brought the bag of warmth back to the earth.

WHEN *the* BEAR WAKES

"Are those all the stories?" asked the girl.

"That's all for this winter," said the bear, taking the grass and branches from the entrance to his den. "I'm hungry now."

He stepped out into the melting snow and turned himself around.

"What are you doing?" asked the girl.

"I'm seeing if I cast a shadow," said the bear.

"And if you do?"

"Then I have to go back into the cave for a bit longer because winter hasn't ended," said the bear.

"And do you cast a shadow?" she asked.

"Can you see one?"

"No!" said the girl.

"Then it's time to look for the spring," said the bear. "Remember all the stories, now! And remember the best gift of all."

And he stomped off down the hillside, leaving only a trail of bear footprints to show he had ever been there.

Sources

WHILE THE BEAR SLEEPS
It was a hard job keeping the bears out of the book! When you write about winter, they want a slice of the action because this is their time of dreaming. I warmly acknowledge the help of Tessa Strickland in interpreting these dreams.

THE WINTER CABIN
In this old Russian story, the five animals have to use their wits to survive attempts on their lives: both men and wild animals want to eat them up. By banding together, they find a solution to their dilemma, acquiring a fearsome reputation in the process. The midwinter season abounds with stories and folk customs about animals, who seem to reveal their special powers in the depths of winter.

A GREAT MIRACLE HAPPENED HERE
The story of the liberation of the Holy Land from the persecutions of Antiochus is the stirring tale which inspired the festival of Hanukkah. You can read the full story in any Bible which includes the Apocryphal books of Maccabees.

THE BLESSING OF THE ANGELS
Christmas Day celebrates the birth of Jesus Christ, a fact which many forget as they hurry to exchange presents and make merry. I have based this story of the Nativity upon the Apocryphal gospel "The Book of James," sometimes known as the "Protoevangelium." These forgotten gospels can give flesh to the often bare accounts in the canonical Bible. The story of Salome and the crown of candles has been incorporated from an Irish legend in which St. Brighid acts as Mary's midwife and distracts Herod's soldiers.

SCHNITZLE, SCHNOTZLE AND SCHNOOTZLE
When the land is laid bare in winter, we like to hear a story about plenty and riches. The Christmas guest in this story brings warmth, color and life to a household that is as bare as Mother Hubbard's cupboard. This story was collected by the veteran storyteller Ruth Sawyer, who went all over the world to hear and collect stories from living storytellers. This one is from Austria.

A RECIPE FOR BETTER TIMES
This Hausa story from Africa underscores the dedication and spirit at the core of Kwanzaa, which is a festival that reminds us of how to live our lives every day. Kwanzaa was instigated by Dr. Maulana Ron Karenga in 1966, to support the cultural heritage of all African Americans. By having self-respect and being aware of how one action can affect everyone else, by honoring every ingredient in life and giving thanks for its special gifts, everyone can contribute to life's rich soup — whoever they are.

BABOUSHKA
This Russian story tells of Baboushka, who loves children and who keeps her house ready for any guest. Her endless journey is begun when the Three Wise Men visit her. This is a story for Epiphany and afterward, when the Three Kings come to the stable in Bethlehem and acclaim Jesus as a king, with royal gifts. In many countries, Epiphany is the time when children receive their gifts and when the deep mystery of Christ's birth is celebrated.

THE BAG OF WARMTH
The return of the sun and of warmth is a preoccupation of all peoples living in the Arctic Circle. As the days get shorter, the fear of an endless winter intensifies. Many tales are told about the shortest day of the year, midwinter day, recounting how the sun is made to return — how it has to be stolen back to rescue the world from endless winter. In this Slavey story from Canada, in place of the sun we have a bag of warmth that is kept by bears who, as we all know, hibernate throughout the winter to emerge in spring.

Bibliography

James, M. R., *The Apocryphal New Testament*, Clarendon Press, Oxford, 1924.
Karenga, Maulana, *Kwanzaa: A Celebration of Family Community and Culture*,
University of Sankore Press, Los Angeles, 1997.
Matthews, John, *A Winter Solstice*, Godsfield Press, New Alresford, 1998.
Sawyer, Ruth, *The Long Christmas*, Viking Press, New York, 1941.
Shepard, Paul and Sanders, Barry, *The Sacred Paw*, Arcana, London, 1992.

BAREFOOT BOOKS publishes high-quality picture books for children of
all ages and specializes in the work of artists and writers from many cultures.
If you have enjoyed this book and would like to receive a copy
of our current catalog, please contact our New York office —
Barefoot Books Inc., 37 West 17th Street, 4th Floor East,
New York, New York, 10011
e-mail: ussales@barefoot-books.com
website: www.barefoot-books.com